AT SCHOOL

By Justine Korman
Illustrated by John Costanza

A Golden Book • New York
Western Publishing Company, Inc., Racine, Wisconsin 53404

 Library of Congress Catalog Card Number: 85-70310 ISBN 0-307-02034-7 / ISBN 0-307-60291-5 (lib. bdg.)
B C D E F G H I J

ROBOTMAN, STELLAR, AND LITTLE OOPS needed love badly. They were so sad that they could hardly move.

Lint hopped around his friends, trying to make them feel better. But they needed love from people. And they needed love from people soon, before their energy ran out entirely.

"We've picked a bad time to need love," said Robotman. "Nobody's around."

Stellar nodded. "All the children are at school."

Robotman looked around with his super telescopic vision.

Stellar sniffed the air for children smells, like peanut butter and crayons.

Oops tried to help, too.

"I hear something!" Robotman said suddenly. "It sounds like a little boy sighing."

Lint was joyful. He jumped up and down, and made sounds of glee.

"There he is," Robotman told Lint.

In the distance Lint could see a little boy sitting alone under a weeping willow tree.

Robotman heard the boy sigh even more sadly than before.

Lint ran as fast as he could. A breeze lifted him up and swept him along.

Lint landed before the surprised little boy.

"Wh-who are you?" the boy asked hesitantly.

Lint handed the boy his card. Printed plainly on it was the name Lint.

"I'm Jason," the boy said.

With noises and gestures, Lint told Jason about his friends. Jason agreed to help them. So off they went on Jason's bicycle, with Lint clinging to the handlebars and pointing the way.

Jason could not resist hugging the robots. Robotman, Stellar, and Oops quickly revived.

"Open the door in my chest," Robotman told the amazed little boy. "Now program my heart, and I will be able to read your thoughts."

Jason touched Robotman's heart. "I *knew* you were sad!" Robotman said. "And now I know why."

"Tell us!" said Stellar and Oops.

"There's a bully who uses his big dog to frighten all the children at school," Robotman began.

Jason added, "We have to give Larry the good parts of our lunches. If we don't, he sics Snapper on us."

"Just let me at that dog!" Oops shouted, punching the air so hard he tripped over his own big feet.

Stellar laughed. "There may be a better way than fighting to solve this problem."

"Let's go see," Robotman said. "Come on, Jason. It's time you went back to school."

The robots and Lint waited in the schoolyard while Jason went to join his class.

"See you at lunchtime," Jason called to them.

"I smell canine," Stellar said nervously. She turned around and discovered that they had been joined by an enormous dog.

"B-b-big d-d-dog," stammered Oops.

Robotman stepped forward bravely and addressed the fierce-looking animal. "Snapper, I presume?"

"Woof," the dog barked.

The robots explained to Snapper that it wasn't nice to frighten children. The dog's eyes widened with surprise. Then he started barking.

Robotman translated. "He says that he's sorry, and that he didn't realize he was being mean. From now on, he wants to use his strength to protect people, not frighten them."

Just then the children started pouring out of the school building. It was lunchtime.

Larry stopped Jason and demanded the cookies from his lunch.

"Don't be afraid, Jason," Robotman called out.

"Look! Robots!" "Who are they?" All the children started to talk at once.

Snapper scampered up to Jason, wagging his tail. The big dog licked Jason's hand.

"Hey, what's going on here?" said Larry.

"These are my friends Robotman, Stellar, Oops, and Lint," said Jason.

"Snapper won't bite any more," Robotman added. "He wants to be friends."

The children laughed and dared each other to pet Snapper. They were full of questions for the robots, too. So Robotman and his friends told all about themselves and Robotland, about wanting to help people and needing love.

Snapper was happy now, with everyone petting him. The robots were happy, with plenty of children to love them. And Lint was happy, too. He got to eat everyone's leftovers.

But Larry was thinking. He was thinking about how happy Snapper looked with all the children petting him, and about how much the other kids seemed to like Jason.

And he thought, “Maybe being nice makes you feel better than being mean.”

Larry thought it might be worth a try.

After lunch, Larry walked over to Jason. "Do you want to play catch?" he asked shyly.

"Well..." said Jason.

"Go ahead," Robotman said. "I think Larry is learning that it's fun to be nice."

"Woof, woof," Snapper barked, and he and the boys ran off to play.